Anniversary Edition

The Bare Naked Book

Written by Kathy Stinson

Illustrated by Heather Collins

Annick Press
Toronto + New York + Vancouver

Annick Press Ltd.

We acknowledge the support of the Canada Council for the Arts, the Ontario Arts
Council, and the Government of Canada through the Book Publishing Industry
Development Program (BPIDP) for our publishing activities.

Cataloging in Publication

Stinson, Kathy
    The bare naked book / written by Kathy Stinson ; illustrated by Heather
Collins. — 20th anniversary ed.

ISBN-13: 978-1-55451-050-4 (bound)
ISBN-10: 1-55451-050-3 (bound)
ISBN-13: 978-1-55451-049-8 (pbk.)
ISBN-10: 1-55451-049-X (pbk.)

    1. Body, Human—Juvenile literature. I. Collins, Heather II. Title.

QM27.S75 2006   j611   C2006-901081-1

Distributed in Canada by: Published in the U.S.A. by:
Firefly Books Ltd.   Annick Press (U.S.) Ltd.
66 Leek Crescent   Distributed in the U.S.A. by:
Richmond Hill, ON   Firefly Books (U.S.) Inc.
L4B 1H1   P.O. Box 1338
                                   Ellicott Station
                                   Buffalo, NY 14205

Printed in China.

Visit us at: www.annickpress.com

To all the lovely little "nudies" in my life – my children, nieces, nephews, and grandchildren – who have shown me over the years that a bare naked body is indeed something to celebrate.

—K.S.

Bodies

Running bodies ... Swimming bodies

Jumping bodies ... Stretching bodies ...

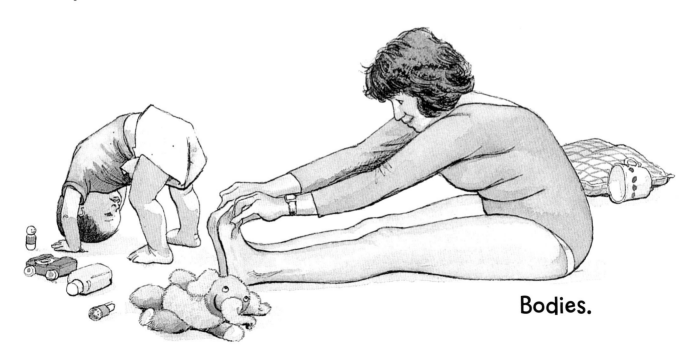

Bodies.

Hair

Dripping hair

Straight hair

Curly hair

Tangled hair

Hair ...

Where is your hair?

Teeth

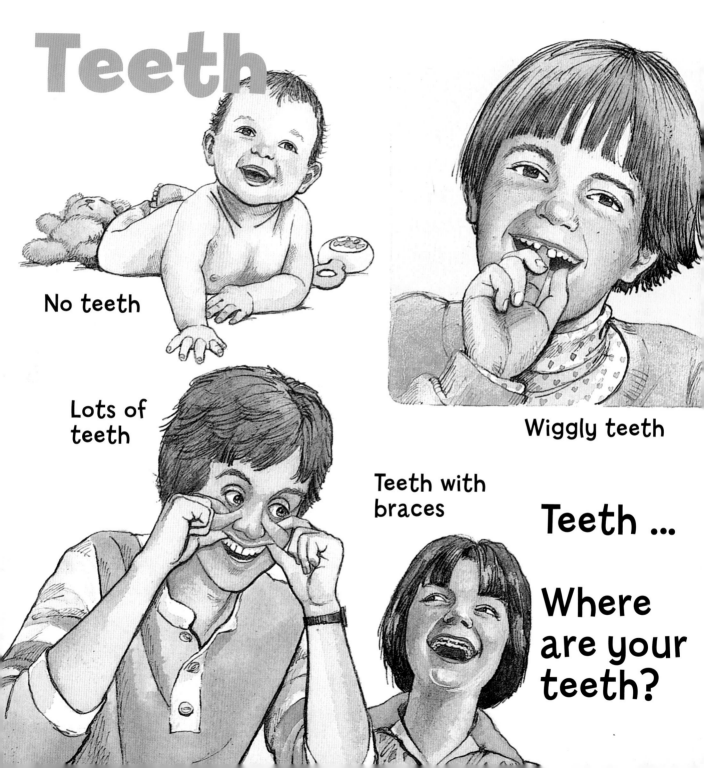

No teeth

Lots of
teeth

Wiggly teeth

Teeth with
braces

Teeth ...

Where
are your
teeth?

Noses

Runny noses

Itchy noses

Blowing noses

Don't pick your nose

Noses ...

Where is your nose?

Tongues

Licking
tongues

Slurping
tongues

Green and purple tongues

Tastes-yucky tongues

Tongues ... Where is your tongue?

Eyes

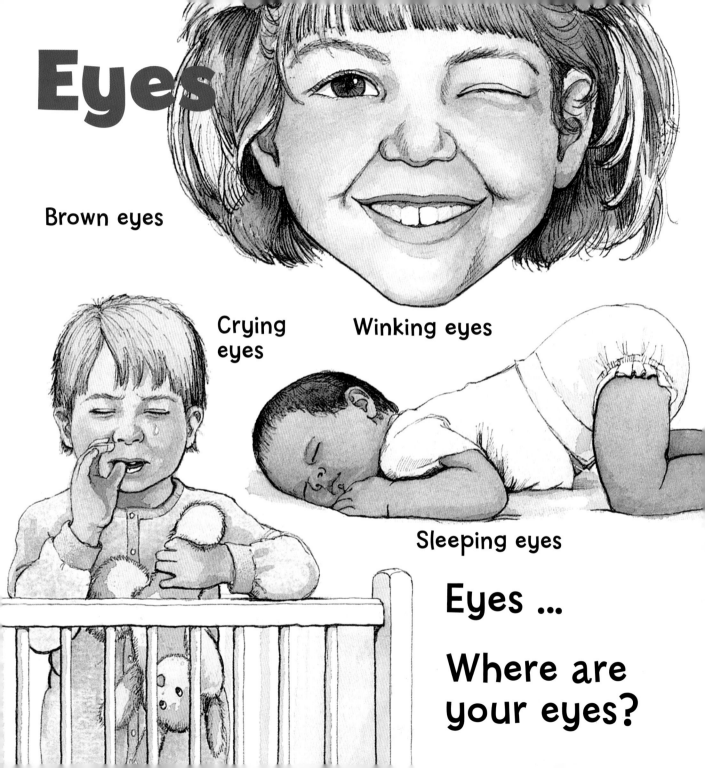

Brown eyes

Crying eyes

Winking eyes

Sleeping eyes

Eyes ...

Where are your eyes?

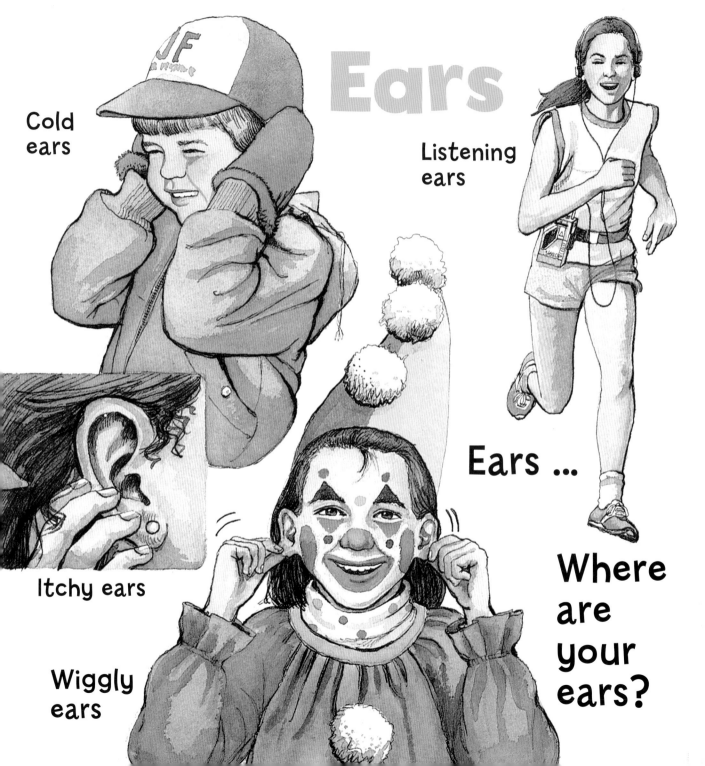

Ears

Cold ears

Listening ears

Itchy ears

Wiggly ears

Ears ...

Where are your ears?

Shoulders

Big shoulders

Hunched shoulders

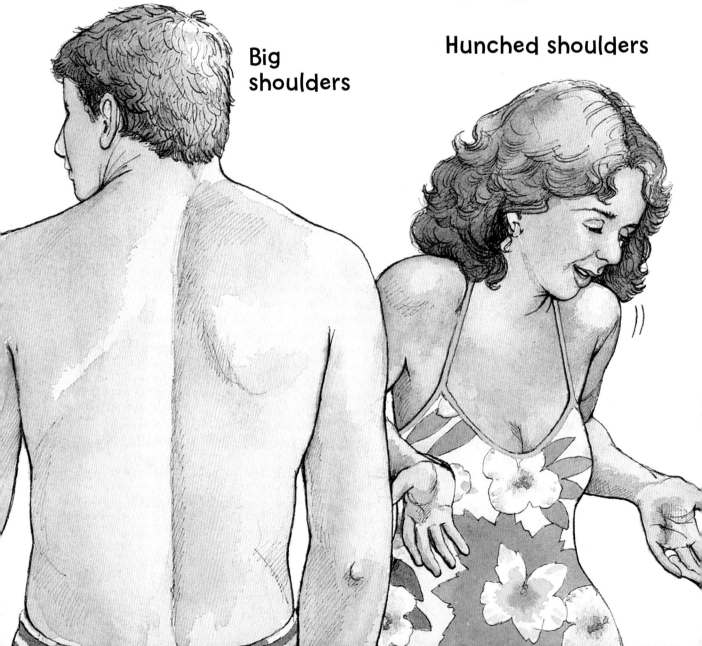

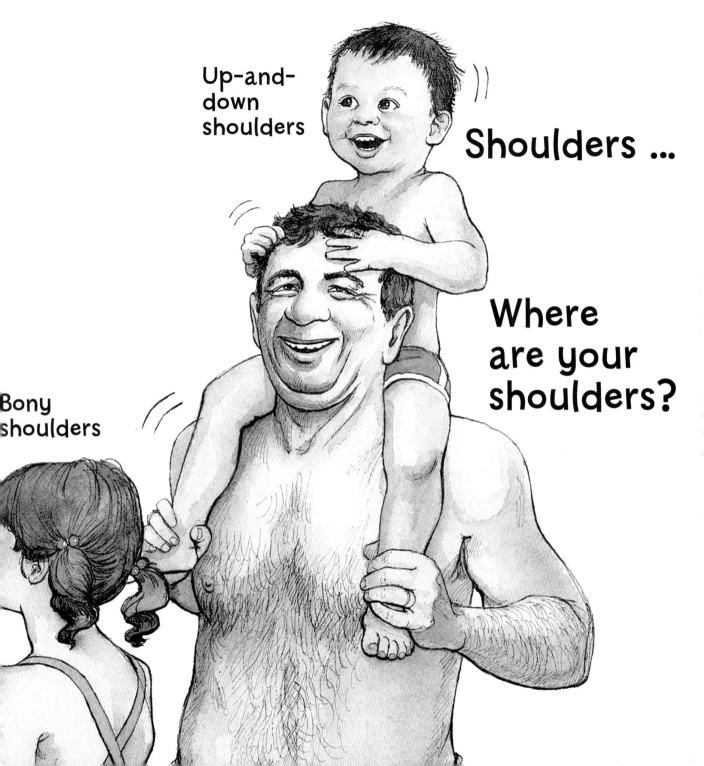

Belly buttons

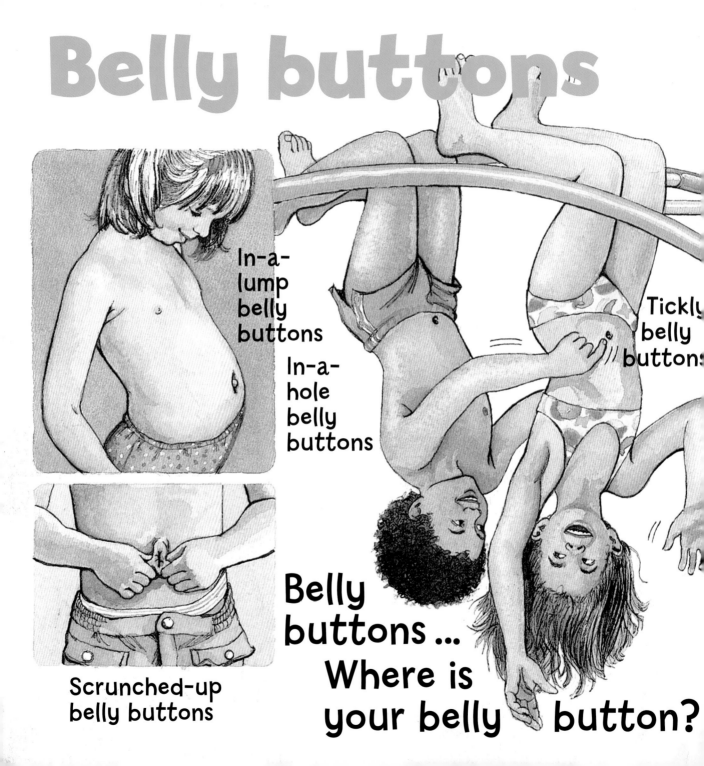

In-a-lump belly buttons

In-a-hole belly buttons

Tickly belly buttons

Scrunched-up belly buttons

Belly buttons... Where is your belly button?

Nipples

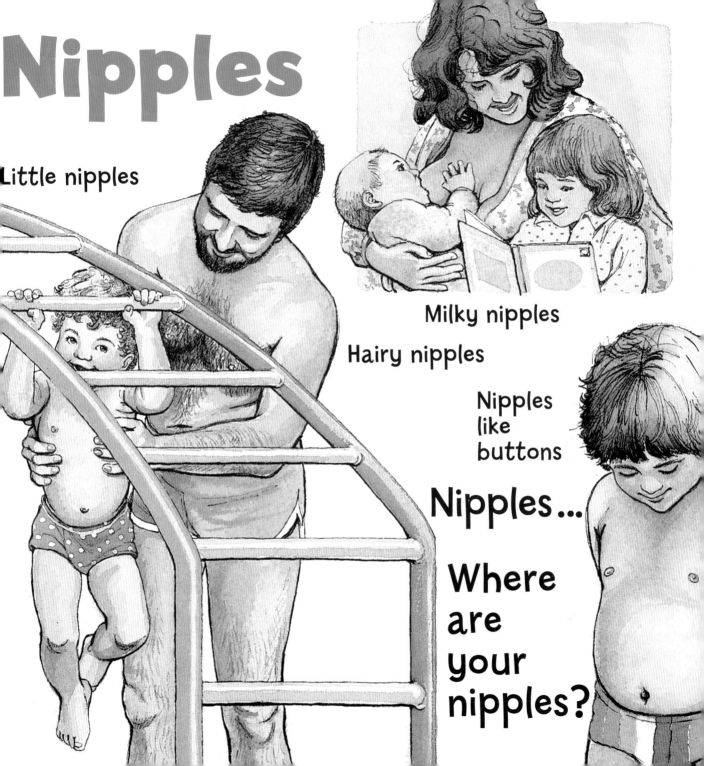

Little nipples

Milky nipples

Hairy nipples

Nipples like buttons

Nipples...

Where are your nipples?

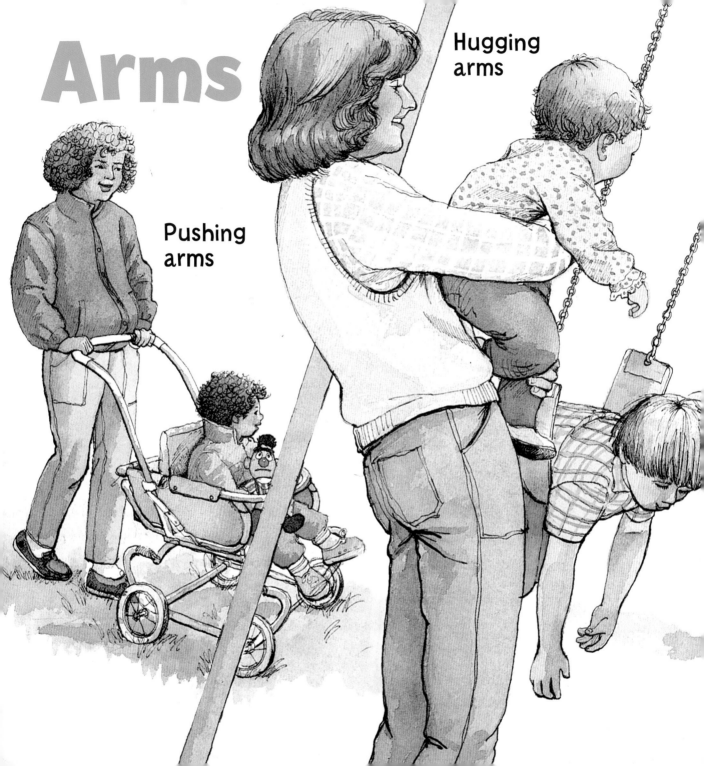

Arms

Pushing arms

Hugging arms

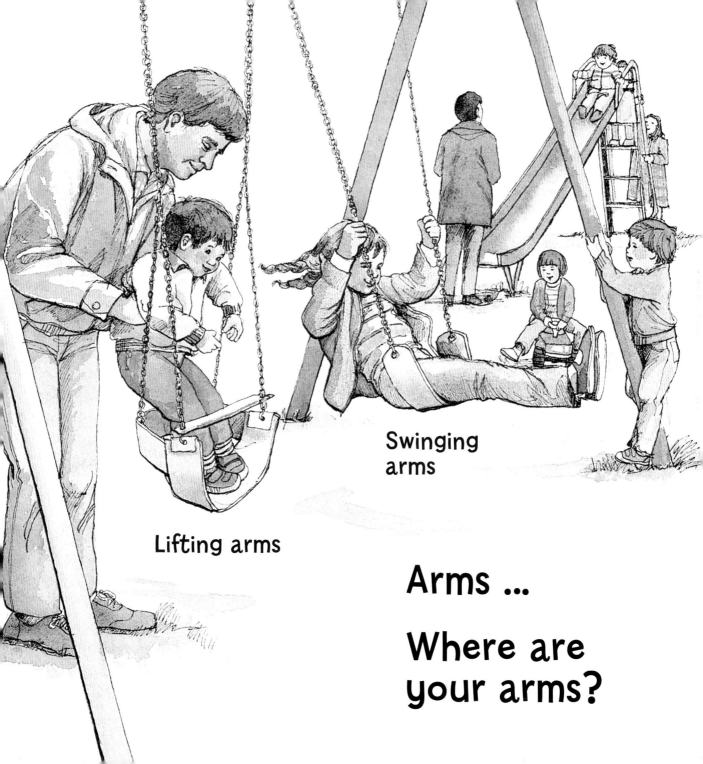

Lifting arms

Swinging arms

Arms ...

Where are your arms?

Hands

Clapping hands

Waving hands

Dirty hands

Holding hands

Hands ...

Where are your hands?

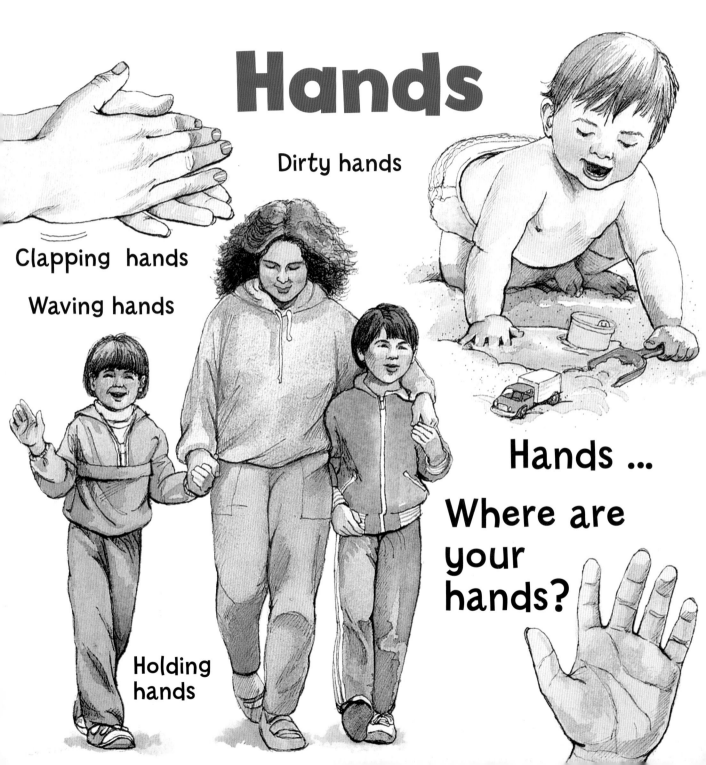

Fingers

Pinched fingers

Poking fingers

Playing fingers

Sucking fingers

Fingers ...

Where are your fingers?

Penises

That's for boys

Penises ...

Where is your penis?

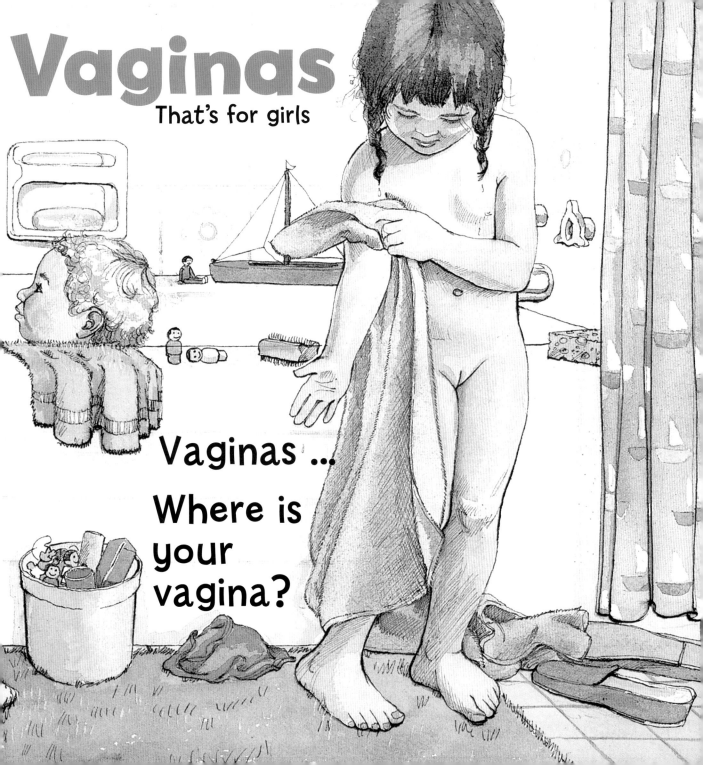

Bums

Standing-up bums

Sitting-down bums

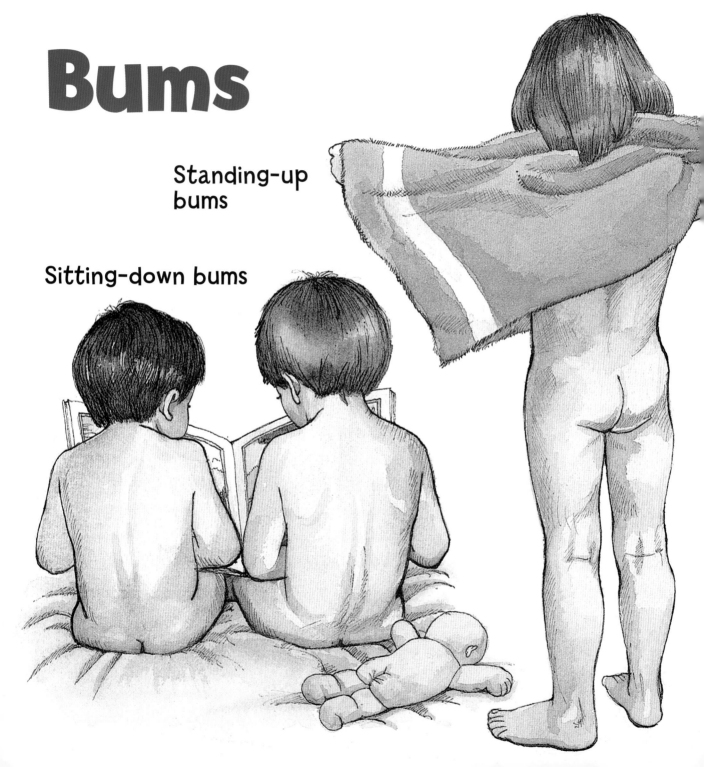

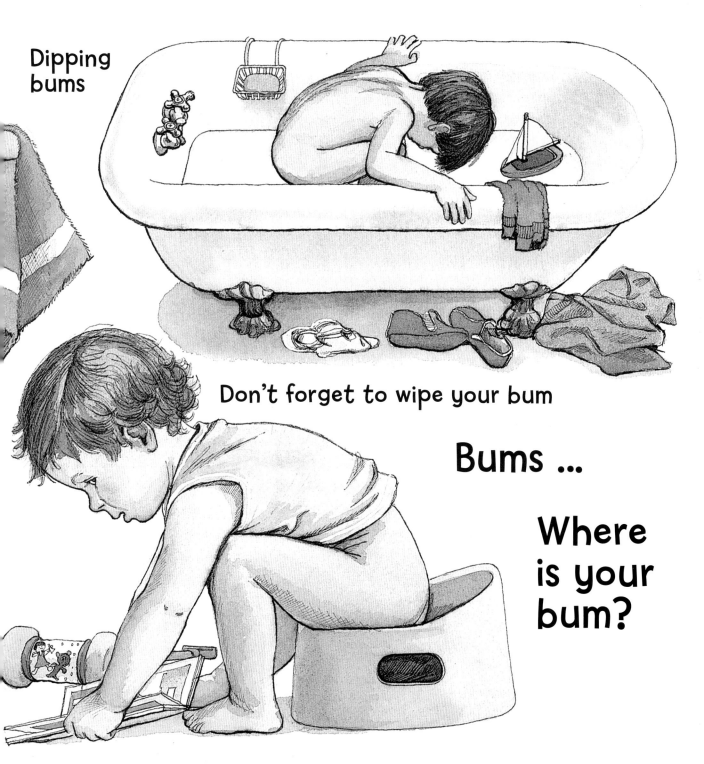

Dipping
bums

Don't forget to wipe your bum

Bums ...

Where
is your
bum?

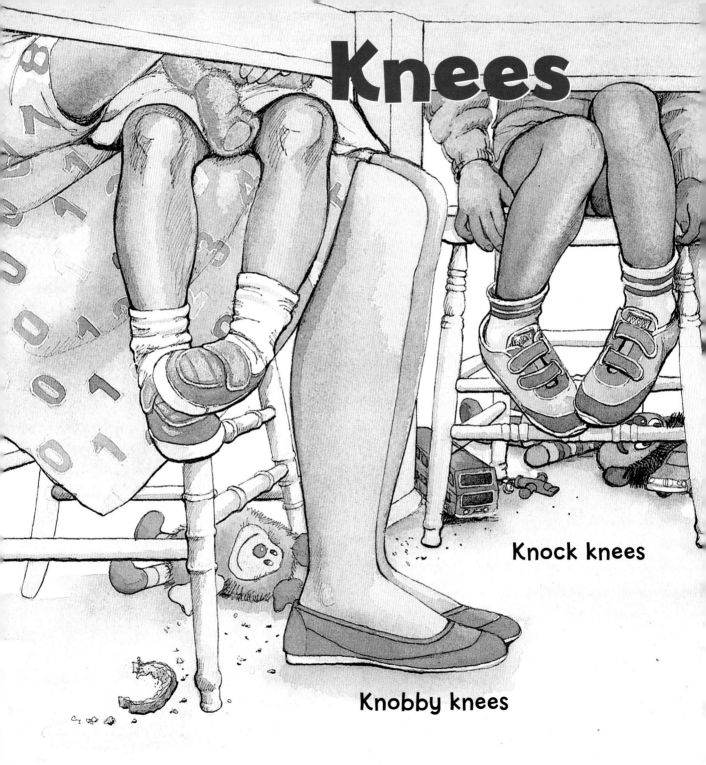

Knees

Knock knees

Knobby knees

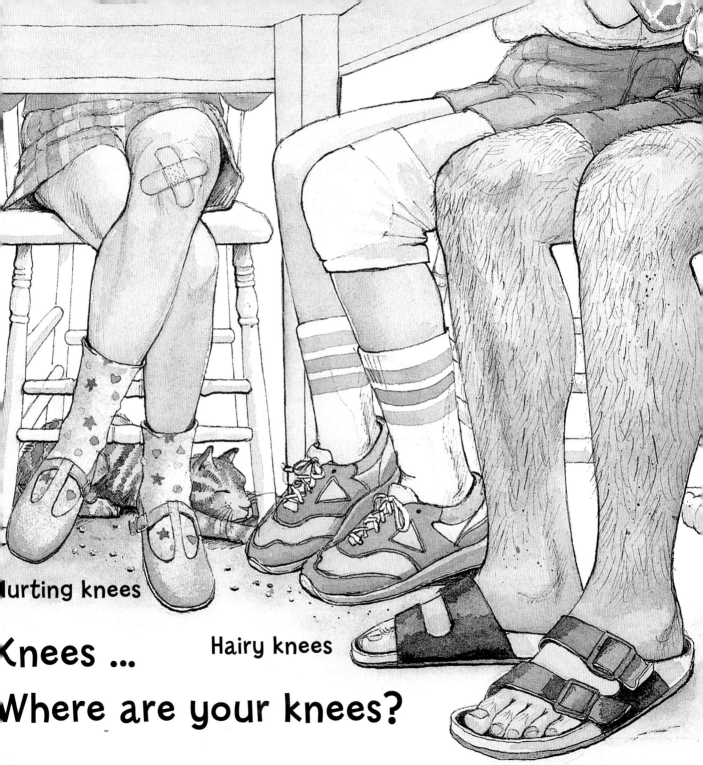

Hurting knees

Hairy knees

Knees ...
Where are your knees?

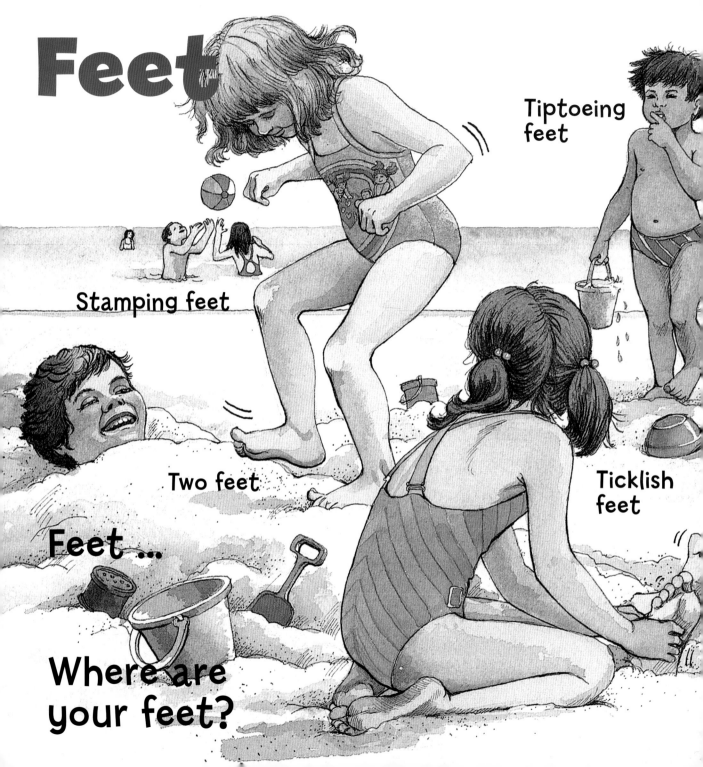

Feet

Tiptoeing feet

Stamping feet

Two feet

Ticklish feet

Feet ...

Where are your feet?

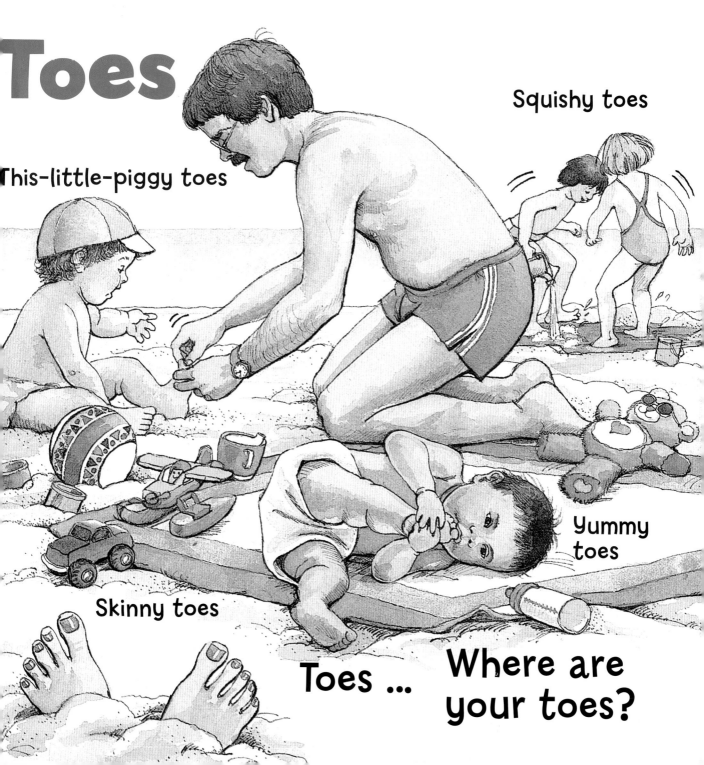

Toes

Squishy toes

This-little-piggy toes

Yummy toes

Skinny toes

Toes ... Where are your toes?

Bodies

Loving bodies

Soaking wet
happy bodies

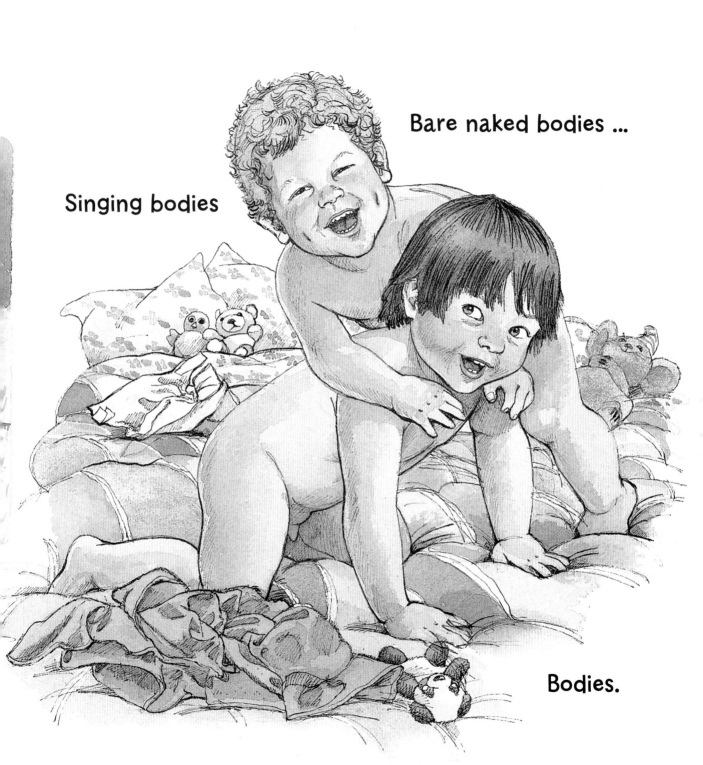

Singing bodies

Bare naked bodies ...

Bodies.

Kathy Stinson

Since the original publication of *The Bare Naked Book*, Kathy has gone on to write many more books for readers from tot-age to teen-age. One of the best things to come out of this book, she feels, is her friendship with its illustrator. Kathy can occasionally be found bare naked at her home near Guelph, Ontario where she lives with editor and teacher, Peter Carver.

Heather Collins

The Bare Naked Book remains a favorite among the many books Heather has illustrated. Its art work continues to make her smile, as it depicts family and friends, all grown up now.

Heather continues to illustrate for young children and divides her time between the shores of Georgian Bay and downtown Toronto with husband and designer, Blair Kerrigan.